ALASKA'S
THREE BEARS

By SHELLEY GILL

Illustrated by SHANNON CARTWRIGHT

Alaska's Three Bears

Text copyright © 1990 by Shelley Gill
Illustrations copyright © 1990 by Shannon Cartwright
Manufactured in China in November 2017 by C&C Offset Printing Co. Ltd. Shenzhen, Guangdong Province

Library of Congress Card Number 90-092102
ISBN 13: 978-093400-711-5 (pbk)
ISBN 0-934007-11-X (pbk)
ISBN 0-934007-10-1 (hc)

PAWS IV
Published by Sasquatch Books
1904 Third Avenue, Suite 710
Seattle, Washington 98101
(206) 467-4300
www.SasquatchBooks.com

For Arnie
my albatross, anchors aweigh!
S.G.

and Gary
my teacher in the wild country,
S.C.

Once upon a time there were three bears...a big white bear, a medium-sized brown bear and a small black bear.

There are three species of bear in North America. Grizzlies used to roam from Ohio to California; now the big brown bears have been driven north onto the last pieces of remote land. Black bear can still be found in forests throughout the U.S. but only in Alaska and Canada can you find all three bears; the grizzly, polar bear and black bear, living in the wilderness we call bear country.

Brown bears stand 6 to 8 feet tall and weigh from 400-1500 pounds depending on where they live and what they eat. Polar bears measure between 8 to 10 feet when they stand on their hind legs. They weigh between 600-1400 pounds. Black bears are the smallest bears, standing 5 to 6 feet tall and tipping the scales at 100-400 pounds.

At the first sign of spring the bears began to wander across the great land known as Alaska. One by one they came to a vast empty delta and it was there that they met each other for the first time.

Modern bears evolved from a family of small, meat-eating, tree climbing mammals called Miacids. The first real bears appeared about 20 million years ago and were about the size of a fox terrier.

The male bear is called a boar. The female is a sow and she is always smaller than the boar. The baby bear is called a cub.

The big white bear was tired because he had traveled the farthest. With spring almost over he decided it was time to head for home. He just grunted when the brown bear asked to go along. The small black bear tagged behind, skipping sometimes to catch up.

All bears were respected by early Alaskan Natives because of the bear's wild nature, their strength and intelligence. The Eskimos believed the polar bear had magical powers. To hunt any bear with a spear took great courage and endurance.

One day, after crossing miles of bald hills, they came to a place where the land met a frozen sea. The snow crunched as they followed a twisted path through mountains and mountains of ice. The sky was icy fresh and it seemed to dip and disappear until it landed in the white glare of ocean.

All bears have an excellent sense of smell. They can also see and hear well but their nose is what keeps them from going hungry. A polar bear can smell a seal up to 20 miles away or under three feet of ice!

Polar bears are meat-eaters. They will smash through sea ice to catch seals and will occasionally eat a young walrus, ducks or whatever washes up on the beach and looks tasty. The stomach of a large bear can hold up to 150 pounds of food at one time!

The big white bear, the medium-sized brown bear and the small black bear saw lots of tiny tracks in the snow.

"Look, an arctic fox!" said the brown bear. They heard a plop and a splash from a nearby hole in the ice. "A ringed seal," whispered the big white bear. Then everything was still.

Arctic fox follow polar bears all winter long eating the leftovers from the bear's kill. The fox has to be quick though or the bear might make a meal of him.

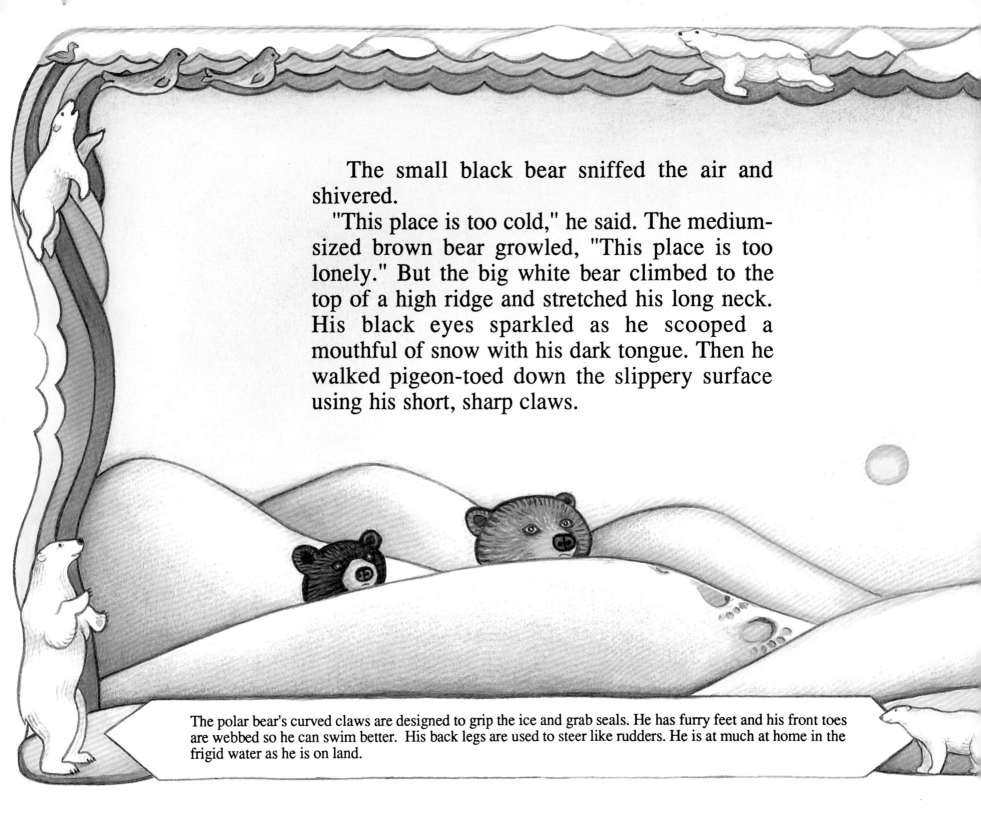

The small black bear sniffed the air and shivered.

"This place is too cold," he said. The medium-sized brown bear growled, "This place is too lonely." But the big white bear climbed to the top of a high ridge and stretched his long neck. His black eyes sparkled as he scooped a mouthful of snow with his dark tongue. Then he walked pigeon-toed down the slippery surface using his short, sharp claws.

The polar bear's curved claws are designed to grip the ice and grab seals. He has furry feet and his front toes are webbed so he can swim better. His back legs are used to steer like rudders. He is at much at home in the frigid water as he is on land.

A polar bear's hair isn't really white but translucent and hollow. Scientists think sunlight is filtered from the outer tips through the hair where it is absorbed by the bear's black skin. So the polar bear is solar heated!

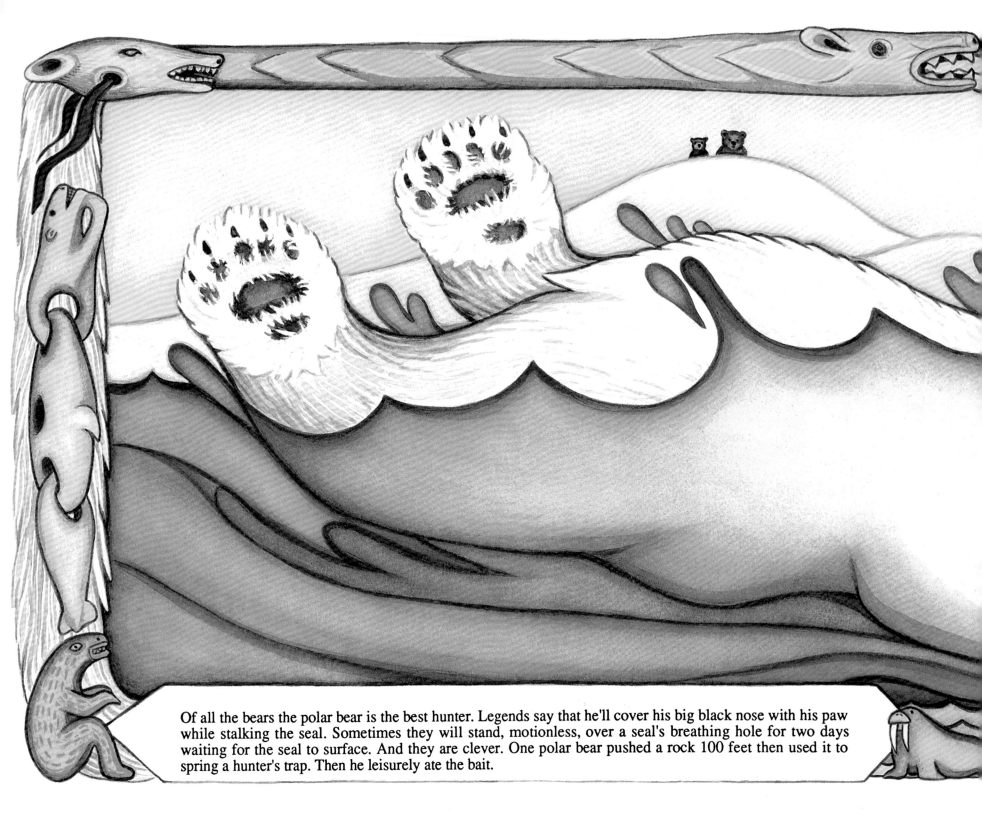

Of all the bears the polar bear is the best hunter. Legends say that he'll cover his big black nose with his paw while stalking the seal. Sometimes they will stand, motionless, over a seal's breathing hole for two days waiting for the seal to surface. And they are clever. One polar bear pushed a rock 100 feet then used it to spring a hunter's trap. Then he leisurely ate the bait.

In the stillness the polar bear looked like he was made of ice and carved by the Arctic wind. His hollow, cream-colored hair kept him warm and helped him blend into the ice-covered land, so he could hunt the ringed seals. He turned to his friends and said, "This place is just right." Then he dove into the frigid water.

The Eskimos called the polar bear "Nanook" which means "great white bear." He is also known as the "Nomad of the North" because he travels with the sea ice. His only enemy, besides man, is the boar walrus which can weigh over a ton. The walrus is a faster swimmer and can kill a polar bear by swimming beneath him and stabbing him with his three foot long ivory tusks.

The small black bear just sniffed as they left the polar bear's home. The brown bear grumbled, "Who could live here? Not me, no, no. I don't like ice. I don't like snow. I don't even like fishin' at 40 below."

The black bear and the brown bear eat whatever they can get. A nice feast might be grass, roots, bugs, berries, fish or a moose calf. During the late summer a brown bear can gobble up to 80 pounds of food a day and gain 3-6 pounds in 24 hours. They spend all summer eating, eating, eating; trying to get enough fat stored for their long winter sleep.

So the two headed south. They crossed tall blue mountains covered with moss and wildflowers. After many miles they came to a big river. Its sharp banks dropped to the silty water. The two bears wandered through a tangle of willows until they came to a stream. The small black bear gulped a drink and scrambled across. But the medium-sized brown bear stopped when he saw a flick of red in the water.

When winter arrives and food becomes scarce the black and brown bears find a hollow or dig a hole where they can sleep out the winter. During hibernation their body temperature and heart rate drop. Only the pregnant sow polar bear hibernates. The male spends the winter hunting on the ice.

A salmon thrashed his tail, kicking up gravel as he swam upstream. The gentle wind ruffled along the hump of gold-tipped hair on the grizzly's back. The bear turned and saw his own tracks, huge and swirled with wrinkles. Suddenly he lunged at another salmon, trying to pin the fish down with his big paw. His claws, long and curved, were as perfect for fishing as they were for digging the roots he loved to nibble in the spring.

Brown bears have many names. Generally all coastal bears are called brownies. The smaller interior brown bears are known as grizzlies. Brown bears that live on Kodiak Island are called Kodiak bears. But they are all the same species and all have the large distinct hump of fat and muscle above their shoulders.

Each brown bear develops his own unique fishing style. Some wait patiently for the fish to swim by and then pin him down with their paw. Others dive into the water, grabbing the fish in their jaws. Another method is called snorkeling. The bear walks up the river with his head under water, holding his breath. When he sees a fish he grabs it in his long, sharp teeth.

Brown bears range in color from almost black to all different shades of brown to white. Some are called silver-tips because the ends of their hair look like they are dusted with a fine coating of frost. Scientists believe the polar bear evolved from the light colored brown bear.

The small black bear groaned. "The ground is too hard here. This place is not home. There are no berries, no forests to roam."

But the grizzly heard a raven calling and saw a caribou prance by on the other side of the stream. There were ground squirrels to chase and roots to dig. "This place is just right," he told the small black bear. And he started upstream, following the salmon.

Early Arctic travelers called the brown bear "the great one" actually fearing to mention his name. Except for man, the brown bear is the ruler of his territory. He may look slow but a brown bear can outrun a horse! Charging brown bears can sprint up to 40 miles an hour for short distances.

The small black bear lumbered away with his head down. His last friend was gone and he was still a long way from home. He wandered through the summer, lonely and sad, until he came to the edge of a deep forest. In the cool autumn shade he stopped at a stump to dig for bugs with his curved, narrow claws. The wood was the color of a shadow, dark gray and blue. It matched his glossy fur and it made him feel better to know that he could hide in the forest and be safe.

The black bear's sharply curved claws are ideal for tree climbing. Black bears also have bare feet; the leathery soles give them traction on a tree's rough bark. Brown bear cubs can climb trees too but as they get older they become too heavy.

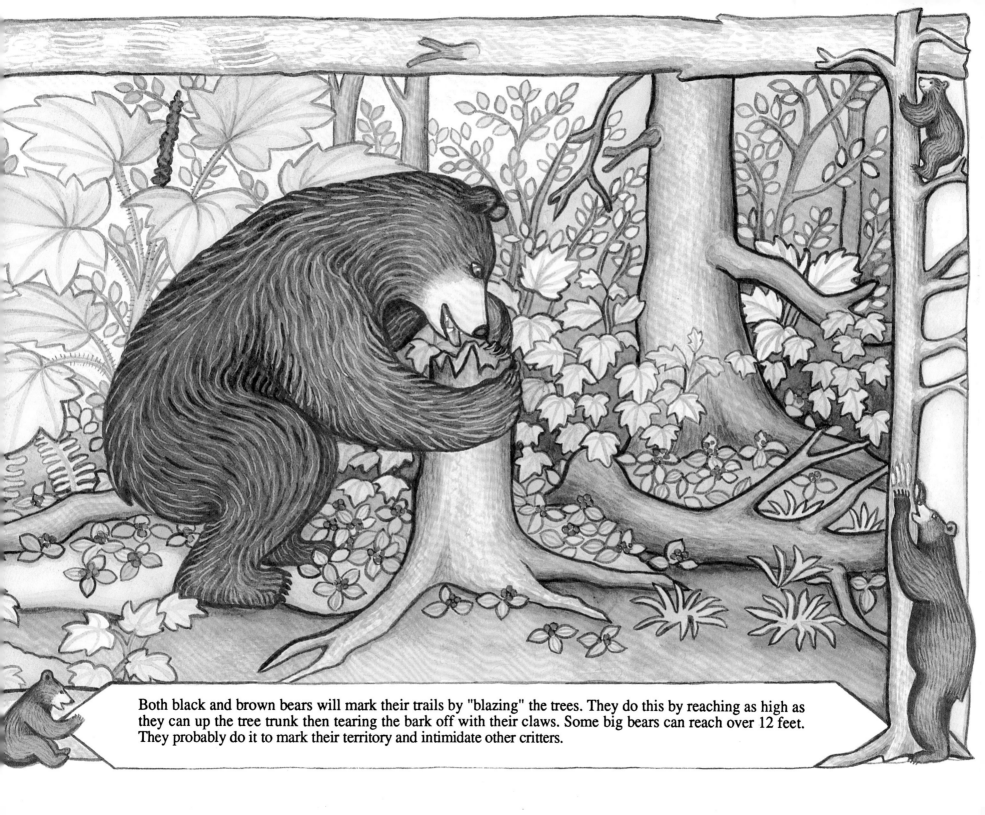

Both black and brown bears will mark their trails by "blazing" the trees. They do this by reaching as high as they can up the tree trunk then tearing the bark off with their claws. Some big bears can reach over 12 feet. They probably do it to mark their territory and intimidate other critters.

The black bear climbed a nearby tree. He heard the friendly chatter of the magpies and smelled the spruce trees. He saw a bull moose and a red fox. He liked the soft moss at the foot of his tree, and the way the light swam through the tall branches.

Black bears can range in color from jet black to bleached blonde. Some have white spots, others are the color of cinnamon. In Southeast Alaska there are some blue-gray bears that are called glacier bears. Most black bears have brown muzzles and all have big ears.

Bears can raise Cain in a wilderness cabin. They'll bite into everything ...books, pencil sharpeners, tin cans. They'll eat paint, chain saw oil and some seem to enjoy the taste of battery acid. They can tear down a food cache, break down doors and have even wrecked airplanes.

Black bears don't like to leave the safety of the forest but sometimes you can find them in alpine areas just as brown bears can be found in the forest. The black bear must be on constant guard if he shares territory with a grizzly. The bigger brown bears will kill and eat their smaller cousins.

As he scrambled down he spotted a clearing where the ground was dappled in red and blue. Berries grew so thick his mouth watered. The smallest of Alaska's bears ran to pick the blueberries, cranberries and a currant or two. He nibbled and gobbled and gulped. Suddenly it was all familiar, like a dream he had dreamed before. "This place is just right!" he said.

All bear cubs are born while the sow hibernates. A litter of two cubs is most common. They are born blind and weigh about a pound. The brown and polar bear cubs stay with their mothers for two winters after their birth. Black bear cubs leave after one winter so a black bear sow can have a new litter every other year. Black bears have survived in areas where brown bears have been wiped out because there are more of them and they can adapt to a variety of habitats.

Bears have very strong homing instincts and seldom leave their home range. Biologists have transplanted them hundreds of miles away only to find the critters back where they began. One brown bear even swam 10 miles to get home. Depending on food sources black bears can live happily in a 2 square mile area. Brown bears range from 6 to 130 square miles while polar bears will range over a 45,000 square mile area. The home range of a male is usually a lot bigger than the female's.

Now, each spring when the light lingers in the sky, when the geese fly north and the flowers bloom, the three bears come out to wander. They may cross mountains or sail an iceberg out to sea but no matter how far Alaska's bears roam they can always find their way back home.

In real life Alaska's three species of bears don't mingle much. One exception is when there is an abundance of food in one place, like a salmon spawning stream or a beached whale. Then bears will congregate in large groups. Bears are usually solitary critters unless it is mating season or a sow is traveling with her cubs. A sow with offspring is very protective and will attack if she feels her cubs are threatened. But she has a good reason to be fearful. Given the opportunity a boar will kill and eat her cubs.

TEACHER RESOURCE GUIDE

Create a list of famous bears (Goldilocks' three, Smokey, Winnie the Pooh, Gentle Ben, etc.) Have kids add to the list throughout the year.

Discuss concept of species. Look at classification. Find a species of an animal and write a "Three _____" story. Include some of the facts found through research.

Use the Venn diagram (graphic organizer) to compare and contrast facts about three bears in a story (what each eats or how they get their food).

Investigate animal tracks. Each student could become an authority on one set of tracks. Go to a nature area to look for tracks or make up a track story using potato print tracks and mural paper.

Use data from book to teach children about graphs. Double bar graphs can be used to show information about height and weight of three bears.

Investigate family names of animals besides boar, sow and cub. Cut out animals and write name on each; display on classroom wall.

Research the bear in myths and legends. How did different cultures view the bear throughout time? How did they use it or protect themselves against it?

Show geographic locations of the different bears; cut out small examples and place on world map to show habitat.

Investigate hibernation.

Explore danger of extinction that bears face. Tongass in Alaska, loss of habitat in United States; investigate ways that kids can help save the bear. . . see Emmy Award winning video THE BIGGEST BEARS by Daniel Zatz (order from 1-800-807-PAWS).

Create a mural to show the adventures of the three bears; students to work on the three distinct habitats and then add the details (other animals; bear eating, etc.) **note: the last page in book shows the three habitats to get the mural started.

Go on a "bear hunt". . .ask students to bring in pictures, facts, articles, books and any information they can find on the topic; - spend some time each day allowing students to be on the hunt; at the end of the reading ask what they "captured" in the way of interesting facts.

How did people perceive the bear throughout history? Did it affect the way the bear was treated? What laws are there to protect bears? What evidence can students find that shows the mistreatment of this animal?

Visit a zoo. . . .make arrangements to have one of the zookeepers come and talk to the class about the care and handling of the bear; let kids send their questions to the zoo in advance of the trip so that resource person will be prepared.

Find out how the constellation of the bear was developed; read the story to the class; have them create a bear constellation; use dark paper and a paper punch or gold stars; use terms Ursa major and Ursa minor.

Bear country is wild country. If you live here you have to beware. Bears can have toothaches or just wake up grumpy. They can be unpredictable and downright dangerous.

If you are in bear country:

~Never feed the bears
~Make noise to let them know you are around
~Don't camp on a bear trail
~Keep your food outside of your tent and up a tree
~Burn or pack out all of your garbage
~Use a flashlight at night

Remember, the bears were here first. Please respect their home. It would be a shame to lose them.

We would like to thank **Jack Lentfer**, biologist and bear expert extraordinaire, for sharing some of what he knows about these wonderful critters.

THE ALASKA ABC BOOK

KIANA'S IDITAROD

MAMMOTH MAGIC

ALASKA MOTHER GOOSE

THUNDERFEET

DANGER – The Dog Yard Cat

ALASKA'S THREE BEARS

NORTH COUNTRY CHRISTMAS

COUNT ALASKA'S COLORS

IDITAROD CURRICULUM

SWIMMER

DENALI CURRICULUM

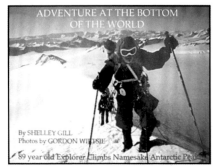

ADVENTURE AT THE BOTTOM OF THE WORLD

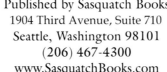

STORM RUN

Titles available from PAWS IV

Published by Sasquatch Books
1904 Third Avenue, Suite 710
Seattle, Washington 98101
(206) 467-4300
www.SasquatchBooks.com